The Irritatingly Erotic Adventures Of Charles McBride

Alan L Williams

This book is dedicated to

Martin Brand

and to

Douglas Davies

**With thanks to
Suzanne Blumsom,
Emma Hunt
and
Antonio Furcas.**

All Aboard…

The afternoon train curved through the villages dotting the railway line between Pisa and Forte Dei Marmi. Charles had taken this train exactly nineteen times in his life; first as a child with his parents, then with the love of his life and now, at fifty, alone.

Pisa was a two-hour flight from London; a hop on and hop off convenience. Within three and a half hours of closing his front door, he was seated at his usual table outside his favourite little café in Garibaldi Square at the side of the Arno, people-watching with a beer - as was tradition.

By his second beer, he had already let out a contented sigh relinquishing all the stresses and concerns of London, and like that, they were gone. Here he felt as relaxed as a local, tucked away in the shadows, invisible to the world. Sometimes the owner of the little establishment recognised him and sometimes not; he preferred it when he didn't. Today the old Italian was busy but he looked over, acknowledged him with a nod and then was gone.

The people of the world wandered by, their faces tilted up to the tall buildings; lovers of all ages holding hands, giggling girls lusting after tight-T-shirted boys, women in tottering high-heels grappling with uncooperative dogs, men in diamond ankle bracelets, teenagers in big boots, ugly old women in even uglier French shoes. Noisy cases battled with cobbles, bikes wooshed by like darts from blowpipes, babies with fat bouncy cheeks leaned over the sides of their jiggling prams.

"Life is in the details," his mother had told him. She had told him that a lot during her final years. She had also called him Melissa, but that was the luck of the draw with Alzheimer's.

This little bar he considered to be one of his own life's most enjoyable details, along with his favourite leather carryall set down at his side and the lucky green boxers folded neatly within it. When his second beer was finished, he hoisted up a heavier, older frame than had sat there the last time, then stretching his back, stepped out beneath the sun, crossed the bridge and made his way towards his awaiting train.

He travelled light, best clothes only; Forte Dei Marmi was the playground of the super-rich and fashion's elite, so it was crucial to wear the latest designs (or the old ones which Charles considered classic and therefore superior to new). Once, the little seaside resort had been the holiday destination of royalty, celebrity and new money. Then for a decade all the tourism had faded away, leaving it forgotten about and abandoned while the rich went back to Monte Carlo and those damned little islands off the top of Venezuela where they were guaranteed to be photographed and gossiped about. But now Forte Dei Marmi was back on top again, its little streets home to the most exclusive and expensive boutiques, in which the sale of one dress a fortnight was enough to keep each afloat, pay the wages and turn a profit.

Michelin Star restaurants, delicatessens and al fresco cafés made up the rest of the town. And yet, despite having no interest in fashion and not looking forward to dining alone, Charles could barely contain his excitement to get back to the little place he had frequented since childhood. He stepped on to the train eagerly, blissfully unaware that something was to happen on this journey which would very much upset his applecart.

At Viareggio, an extraordinarily fashionable, handsome man - excited, energetic and young, stepped on to the train and put down an expensive multicoloured designer leather holdall, before offering Charles a broad and genuine smile. Charles shifted in his seat uncomfortably. One could be handsome and possess youth, one could be older and uglier but be rich, therefore superior in that way, but this youth appeared to be both and that cancelled out Charles' entire system of defence. It confronted him with one very specific and uncomfortable thought. "I am old," he said to himself. "I am old and there is nothing I can do about it."

A short distance onward, the train came to a screeching and violent halt, almost hurling the youth into Charles' lap.

"Apologies ladies and gentlemen," snapped an agitated female voice over the speakers, "but it seems we have all become the victims of an unexpected nightmare. Tu! Quello nuovo! Come si dice Lupo in Inglese? È caffè? Ho detto tè! Attento, oh bene mi hai smagliato le calze. Grazie!Grazie mille!" (You! New boy! What is the English for Wolf? Is that my coffee? That's a coffee for a *weak person, do I look weak? Careful! Oh great, you've laddered my tights. No - Thank you! Thank you very much!)*

She paused before assuming a clipped and polite public voice then continued.

"I'm afraid the train has hit an Apennine wolf, the national animal of Italy. We've abandoned the eagle now apparently," she muttered with irritation. "The animal is still alive, which is unfortunate because it means that we will be doing all we can to save it and are not allowed to throw it from the track."

She flicked noisily through the pages of a book and read monotonously. "The species is protected because of its unique mtDNA haplotype, and, of course, because of its distinct skull shape, as well as being Italy's favourite animal - first I've heard of it. So please make yourselves comfortable. I will keep you updated with our progress."

"I don't know if you understood," said the handsome Italian man turning to him. "Her accent was quite strong and regional but I can translate for you if you…"
"Grazia," Charles replied with a shake of his head and an appreciative smile, "but I understood. I speak Italian."

The younger man nodded, then suddenly let out a cry of genuine excitement. He was pointing to Charles' treasured carryall. "We have exactly the same leather bag!"

Charles creased his brow and stared at the overexcited youth. Is he a youth he wondered? What age were youths exactly? Everyone under twenty-nine looked like a youth since he'd turned forty-five and avoided making comparisons on his attractiveness with others. He watched the young man pick it up and study it carefully from all angles, even its underneath.

"Mine is three years old, yours must be… The last time they made these was thirty-seven years ago. I had mine made from pictures of it that were in a society travel magazine I'd kept since I was eleven and here it is, the genuine article."

He was truly beautiful, Charles observed, studying his healthy, sparkling eyes, broad and effortless white smile, glossy dark hair and tight tanned skin with its enviable, youthful elasticity, all of it set off splendidly in tight, fashionable clothes. He had to be about… "How old are you?" he asked outright; you were able to do this when you got older without it seeming rude.

"Twenty-one," the youngster replied.

In just twenty-one years this strapping six-foot lad had evolved from an embryo the size of a pin-prick. Biology was astounding. Charles nodded to himself.

"We must have the only two remaining bags in existence," the stranger continued.

"The only one," Charles corrected him. "Yours is a fake."

"Name your price, anything. I will buy it from you."

"Not at any price," the Englishman replied with alarm. "This is my lucky bag, my trusty travel companion. Now put it down, you're going to crease my shirts."

The boy nodded and put it back at the older gentleman's feet, then throwing his long, slim body back into the seat opposite like a bored and impatient child, he turned his head towards the window.

Italian men; Charles McBride had spent his life admiring their style, their fiery passion, effortless masculinity and tender, respectful concern. Apart from their fondness for bright colours - which was terribly un-British - and their tight, tight trousers - which made it possible to tell whether the person you were talking to was circumcised or not - Charles wanted to be just like them.

Penises of all shapes and sizes were put carelessly on display in Italy, he had observed over the years. Italian men did not care who noticed their cobblers - and why on earth should they? he reasoned. Though, many a time when he had been confronted with them at eye-level as waiters took his order or barmen brought drinks with their father's gifts practically resting on his shoulder, he had often had to fight back his propensity to complain.

Even now, with this bag-coveting twenty-one-year-old Charles was confronted with it. The nearly-a-man was sitting, head thrown back, legs splayed, t-shirt tugged upwards revealing a taut, tanned, fatless stomach with wiry dark hairs around the well of his navel sweeping down in a hypnotic line to the soft white cotton of his briefs that showed above some low-cut green cotton trousers. Charles' own stomach hair had lost its colour and become as thin and wispy as invisible thread over a decade ago. And there, between the stranger's legs and plainly on show - effortlessly unarranged genitalia.

This manner of dress was not about going to any great effort to show off impressive equipment, it had never been about that for Italians. It was almost as if they weren't aware of it. As much thought was put into randomly cramming their sausage and eggs into a tight trouser as was given to tying the laces on a pair of Sebagos with a glass of wine in the other hand and a cigarette in your mouth while passionately disagreeing with someone in a bar. Throw them in, zip it up, off you go, done. The human body, it is what it is.

Charles looked up from the stranger's crotch to the eyes that had been watching him study it.

"You like?" he asked sarcastically. Charles shook his head. "Excuse me - I was lost in thought."
"About my penis?"
"No, I am not interested in that."
"But you are gay?"
"No, not at all."
The youth nodded, took out his cigarettes and offered him one.

Charles declined. It never failed to surprise him that despite the EU ruling, Italians still smoked in bars and restaurants and on trains. It was rather liberating and relaxing watching them. It was as if they were sticking their fingers up to the rest of Europe and saying we are Italy, you can all piss off.

"Then why do you study it?" the youth asked, pointing between his legs.

During Charles' thirties he had once attempted to reinvent himself as an Italian man, liberating himself with open shirts, dressing in tight trousers, putting it all on display. He found that in Italy, no one looked, no one cared. On his arrival home in Britain, a woman pointed him out to the police at the airport and he was taken to one side then threatened with the charge of gross indecency. So that was the end of that.

Now he looked at the youth, stuck for a suitably brief explanation.

"I think that secretly, you like men," the twenty-one year old grinned, "but you grew up in an age when it was not ok so you got used to denying it."
But Charles hadn't. Charles had no interest in other men's genitalia at all.

"Ladies and gentlemen, unfortunately the Apennine wolf is still alive. The wolf, of course, is Italy's national animal. Some believe that the werewolf was inspired by the wolves of the Apennine region. I do not know this as a fact. I have zero interest in the wolves in horror books or films. In Italy, you will of course know that the wolf saved Romulus and Remus from the river and along with that… woodpecker - who fed them - and all of that.

"The wolf we have here today is in extreme pain but we cannot kill it which to my mind is logic, so I ask to you people in several languages, here today, are you a vet or a doctor or something like that to help. Thank you very much."

"Perhaps we should walk," the young man suggested. "It can't be far to the nearest road and we could share a taxi."
"And risk the werewolves out there?" Charles asked but the youth did not understand the joke and stared at him blankly.
"Where are you staying?" he asked.
"In Forte, at the Imperial, same hotel every visit. Same room too, 312, every time."
The youth nodded. "And you go there alone or to meet with a wife or friends?"
"Alone, my wife died several years ago - well not died, but we divorced."
"I see. You were unfaithful?"

"No. No! She was."

"You were too lazy to also be unfaithful?"

"Lazy?"

The man nodded. "You are fat. Fat men are terrible lovers. The bigger the fat-load, the further away from sex they become."

"That's not true I…"

"It is true. You may trust me on this. Fat men can't get the hips in tight. Fat stomachs push the lover away. There is no rough, no tumble because they have to ease themselves into position or the fat will pull them off balance and make them fall. Safe and comfortable sex only, slow and calm. They treat the person they have sex with like an object to be positioned into the perfect pose that suits their awkward bodies. Made to bend over, made to kneel, can't sit on top because you don't like your fat chest to be seen and the weight makes you breathe too hard. Trust me, fat people, bad sex. Fat people need sex frames, like walking frames but for a different type of manoeuvring!"

Charles stared at the other man in amazement.
"And this information comes from where?"
"I dated a fat once. She liked to be in control. She didn't really, but pretending to like control made it less obvious she was awkward and stiff. She also liked to take control in a different way, if you get my meaning."
Charles laughed, though he was not sure why.
"I like your Britishness. All the unspoken horrors you feel about what I have said to you is displayed with the flicker of an

awkward smile that lasts no longer than a millisecond."

"I think we should change the subject."

"You brought the subject up."

"Sex? How?"

"By staring at my penis like you are appreciating art or trying to burn it in your memory because I'd notice if you brought out a camera."

"I assure you I was not!"

"And I assure you Mr England, that at some point in your future, which had better be soon because you are progressing quickly in age…"

"I am fifty!"

"You are an OLD fifty."

Charles stared and thought, paused and thought some more then looked back at him, searching the young man's expression for sincerity before looking down, but not down for too long, he looked up and right again - fast.

"One day at some point in your future," the Italian continued, "you will have a homosexual experience."

Charles rolled his eyes. "Oh God, they all say that. Homosexuals have fancied me at twenty, thirty, forty… It's nothing new. I have no interest in males."

"And I would like to remind you that this afternoon you have been subliminally inviting me to your bedroom, room 312 at the Imperial."

"I did no such thing. That was merely conversation. This is why homosexuals are annoying," he said waving a finger, "they think everyone is gay."

The handsome, young Italian gave him a broad and wicked grin, revealing strong, dazzling teeth.

"I am teasing you. I knew from the baggy grey trousers you were not a gay man. I could also tell that you have given up on sex, lost the hunger for it. You are fifty and fat and English, you want to sit down and watch the world go by while you sip tea and wait for death." Charles stared at him furiously.
"I do not wear tight trousers because I am fifty and because… because…."
"Because your ball carrier-bag is now stretched and long and floppy like an elephant ear spread out and sticking to your legs so in tight trousers it looks confusing and odd?"

Charles was outraged. "NO! And before you suggest it, my penis is not tiny either, nor is it odd-shaped or down to my knees and yes it still works. It is still a source of immense pleasure. Now can we please stop talking about our genitals?"

"Men never talk about their genitals do they?" the youth mused, throwing his cigarette out of the window. "They think it makes them sound bisexual or curious."

Charles rolled his eyes and sighed.

"When a man talks about his genitals, the people he is talking to look at him suspiciously, as if there is some ulterior or subversive motive behind his words. Genitals are as real and as much a part of the body as the nose or arm or thumb. There is no reason to be shy about talking about them and that is why Italian men do not care if our small, medium or large penises are on display in tight trousers."

Charles eyed him and folded his arms.

"You see, for example, a man displaying a small penis can be selected quite easily from the crowd by a woman who prefers a small penis and so on with the medium and large. Imagine, a beautiful, almond-eyed princess, slim and petite and hopelessly in love with you. At long-last she takes you to her bedroom, pulls down your underwear and oh no, here is the man she wants to keep forever but he has the penis of a horse. She knows herself that her vagina is small and that she has always hoped for a man with an appendage the size and width of a slim packet of mints. She does not want a great heavy pound of sausage that is too big for her."
"Oh for God's sake that's ridiculous! I'm sorry but I have yet to hear of a woman

who actively seeks out a smaller John Thomas."

The Italian laughed "John Thomas! You really are the most unromantic of all races."

"We are all animals. We are driven by a desire for sex, by attraction, breeding, love, company. If a woman falls in love with someone who turns out to have a big sausage, she's not about to dump him, trust me. More than likely she'll post pictures of him in speedos on all of her online profiles and tell everyone multiple times when she is drunk to be the envy of all her friends."

"That, mister English, is sexist."

"Don't be a fool. This almond-eyed woman will find a way. Life is meant to challenge us," Charles replied curtly, irritated with the youth's pop-psychology nonsense.

"I am twenty-one," the Italian persisted. "I have had two good, strong girlfriends. The first, well, we were too young, 16, 17; great sex, lots of fun, exciting arguments and fights but after a year, we changed, as people who are maturing do, so we separated."

Charles filled his lungs with air and let it out irritably.

"The next one, she was older, fatter, she liked to be in control. She liked to put things inside me, you know what I mean, around the back?"

Charles stood immediately and looked through the window. "I am thirsty. Do you think they will be much longer?"

"And you know the first time it hurt very much and as she did it to me I wondered, am I gay now or the woman in this relationship or what am I? What is it? What is going on that I now surrender my body to the woman who wants to be the man and I tell you, the next day I walked like a cowboy, like cowbells swing between my legs because the fire of the ring…"

"Jesus Christ man!" Charles snapped. "Do I need to know this? Do I? I mean why are you even telling me this? Enough! If we have to talk at all, let's talk about the weather!"

"It is July. It is Tuscany. It is sunny. Have you ever…"

"NO I HAVE NOT!"

"Anyway, we are no longer together now and the ring; it gets tight again, you know? Like I'd never…"

Charles snatched up his bag, turned and stormed through the train to find a place he could be alone.

He had been seated there for thirty minutes or so when the voice of the woman on the speakers at last broke the silence.

"Ladies and gentlemen. Thank you for your patience. The Apennine wolf, the national animal of Italy which was hit by our train today, has now been freed from beneath the wheel that was resting on its tail. Unfortunately because it is the national animal of Italy, we were not allowed to cut off the tail and none of us knew how to do it because of the bone and the arteries and the excessive blood loss etc. However, thanks to a helpful passenger, Francesco, the tail has now been removed, the stump bandaged and the wolf has been given the name of Fat Charles."
Charles growled angrily.
"Ladies and gentlemen, we shall arrive in Forte Dei Marmi in four minutes."
"Four minutes? Four bloody minutes!"

Stepping into a taxi, middle-age spread popped two buttons on Charles' shirt revealing the deep well of his navel and the mountainous milky-white bounce all around it. The air was sticky and humid. By the time he had wound down the window, his forehead was already dotted with a galaxy of perspiration balls.

The car hummed along in no great hurry. Life was slower here. It cruised at a sedate pace down the quiet familiar roads, past houses he remembered well, new shops that raised an eyebrow and leafy squares in which contented old men, seated on benches, smoked and read newspapers and watched the world go by. When he was a boy,

Charles had wanted to grow old and be just like them. Now getting old made him terrified of death and was better not thought about at all.

The car moved in to narrower streets and around tricky corners here, entering the busier part of the little town. Already the type of tourist had altered; gone were worn, lived-in clothes and faces, here was the stalking-ground of stick-thin giantesses swishing along the pavements in flowing lime-green silks, of hip-bones jutting out above the rose-pink and clashing sherbet-orange low-cut trouser that everyone wanted, of wide-brimmed hats, red lipstick and protruding-nipples forcing at the material of the tightest of powder-yellow vests while shamelessly distracting everyone.

Glossy, long, ironed hair flew up and around women entrenched in the life-long discipline of maintained slimness. They lowered themselves into the soft padded seats at al fresco cafés, not daring to so much as glance in the direction of the menu and sending back the bread that accompanied their long glasses of Tuppapo - the diet wine. Gucci and Armani and Prada combinations (dress, shoes, bag) brought tuts and disgruntled stares from those purists sporting complete outfits from each label. Here was a land in which women galore scattered themselves in the tree-thrown shade of cafés and sipped on water while their martinis, like business cards, stood untouched awaiting the chime of the next hour.

Sexy, long-lashed, masculine waiters tended to groups of married women out for salads, gossip and flirting. They darted in their white shirts and black trousers among the tables like the fastest of fish but with the most lingering attention. The intricacies of flirting were practiced, perfected and fine-tuned by both customer and waiter in Forte; it was delicious and exciting, as enjoyable as a leisurely game of chess between two equally matched opponents. Every move was considered, each glance filled with tease or rebuke or longing, even the time spent at each café and the length of time between visits came into play. And then of course, there was the tip, where the customer held all the power and the waiter became the plaything of each woman's generosity.

Sometimes, above the cafés, in rooms with crisp white sheets and the lattice windows thrown wide, waiters' aprons fall discarded on the floor, high heels are dropped on to their sides and hairy legs slip between freshly waxed thighs. Expensive skirts are tugged frantically upwards revealing just as expensive underwear, so delicate and magnificent that she is pleased that at long last they are getting the attention they deserve. Then they are tugged down over the hinge of a knee and past a tangle of toes to forever become the reminder of a guilty secret.

The ringing of tills and the clinking of glasses outside blur with the drifting aromas of coffee and cigarette smoke that rise upward. The laughing and giggling at tables just metres away adds to the excitement. It's another hot afternoon and everyone is oblivious to the naked writhing above.

"Tell me you love me!" she demands.
"I don't love you. I don't know you madam."
"Tell me it anyway. Pretend you are the man who is rescuing me from a dead marriage. Call me Yvonne."
"I love you."
"Again!"

He stares into her eyes like the finest and most charismatic actor in town and she becomes flushed with embarrassment and startled by his beauty, by his intensity and by his youth. His hand grabs at her chin and he shakes her head, a little too forcefully than she would have liked but now it feels so much more real. His eyes never once leave hers; they are loving but aggressive and make her want him even more.

"I love you," he breathes into her mouth, his long hair falling on to her face. "I love you with everything that I am. I want you and only you Yvonne. You are mine." And his urgency increases, a little too deep and alarmingly fast, making her eyes widen and her slim fingers grasp at the sides of the mattress. He tugs her legs towards him, widening them so quickly that she feels the sudden panic that accompanies the sharp ache in one of her stiff joints. But he has noticed and becomes gentle and soothing and loving, for a moment at least.

As his mouth descends on to the stiff sensitivity of her left nipple, her hands let go of the mattress and her held-breath suddenly explodes into abandon and noise. She is no longer interested in him but is now fascinated with the sensations of her own body. Running her fingertips over her neck and chest, she teases her breasts with the lightest of touches that make her shiver and her body ripple with goose pimples. She stops thinking at last. Her long, glossy, freshly painted nails slide down her sides, tickling herself, fanning out over her hips as she offers him her neck to bite, which he does, never leaving a mark; he is a professional, this will be a long summer, he does not need drama or husbandly suspicion. Instead, he looks into her eyes and bites her tongue and her lips with a growl so they will be red and hot and she will need to hide them from the women friends who sit down below at their table discussing acceptable lengths of hem. She likes the danger of these risky little reminders.

His thick, intoxicating tongue reacts to the tip of her little sharp one which dances and swirls around it. Her husband no longer kisses her like this. In fact it was probably her that stopped kissing him because she was critical of his dental hygiene - funny the little things that put an end to sex and love. He looks into her eyes again, just as she feels her body begin to spasm and lets out a squeak, then another and grabs his hand, clamping it over her mouth to silence herself. Now he speeds up into a master class of hip movements that he is incredibly proud of and leaves her exhausted and rolling about on the bed, still basking in the sensations she does not want to relinquish yet.

By the time she comes down the stairs he has already served three tables. He looks as pristine as if he has just taken his clothes from the ironing board and smells fresh and soapy. The women who frequent this outdoor café adore him and when she returns to her table of British ladies that she and her husband frequently holiday with, he flicks his napkin, pours her a sparkling water with lemon and ice and asks in his most polite voice "Is everything ok madam? Can I get your table anything else?"

She smiles back to him casually and shakes her head. No one knows, none of the other women seated at her table, even noticed she had gone. They are still watching others to see if these others are watching them - that is the way of Forte Dei Marmi.

In room 312 at the Imperial, Charles dropped his bag down on the bed, threw open the windows and looked out at the sea.
"I am back," he announced with excitement. Then throwing off his travelling clothes, tugging off the British weather socks and the stiff oversized pale blue boxers, he manoeuvred his pale body into the shower to wash the grime of travel away.

It was not his bag.

He realised it the moment he struggled with an unfamiliar zip.

Inside it, neatly folded shirts, t-shirts and trousers in every vibrant and exciting colour imaginable met his mortified gaze. There were trainers and casual loafers and a whole row of expensive aftershaves that he had not even heard of. Panic set in. His credit cards and house keys and all manner of irreplaceable items were gone, even his lucky boxer shorts, spare book and brand new electric shaver.

Had it been deliberate? he wondered. Had the young man who had coveted his original bag switched them at the cost of losing his own belongings or had it been he himself that had snatched it up without looking when he had stormed off? He favoured the latter explanation and thanked God that he had informed the oversexed youth of his hotel and even the room number. He did not remember telling him his name but he must have, he realised, why else would the wolf have been named Fat Charles?

Snatching a glance at himself in the mirror, he studied the overhang of his stomach and tried to suck it in - he was way beyond that. Irritably, he dressed again in the sweat-damp clothes that he had been wearing all day and cursed over and over at the best of his entire wardrobe being in the hands of a stranger. There was only one thing for it, he decided. Until the young lad came to his senses he would remain in the hotel, so without further ado he made his way directly to the bar.

Hardly a head turned in his direction as he walked through the pale yellow room to the counter, even the barman that he'd talked to for years appeared not to recognise him, so he took his drink and tucked himself and his shabby clothes away in a corner. If Yvonne had been with him, undoubtedly by now she would be regaling one table or another with all his faults or some line-up of amusing stories she kept stored away and rehearsed for precisely these occasions. The barman who just moments before had ignored him, would be next to her, her arm around his waist, his barbed compliments making her shriek and slap him. Yvonne liked to be the centre of attention. Without her, the barman who never failed to make a huge fuss of them, had not even recognised him.

Ninety minutes passed, he finished another chapter in the novel he had been reading all week and put it down on the table with a disappointed slap. Those eyes that bothered to look his way either didn't register him or simply looked away again; he was of no interest to anyone it seemed, which was not altogether a bad thing he decided. For a moment he felt like Hemingway sitting in a café in Death In The Afternoon but without the woman who popped into scenes to prompt the plot along. Easing himself up, he headed out to the pool. It was late afternoon, luckily most people were in their rooms agonising over evening-wear, so the area was mostly empty. Charles snatched the opportunity without a second thought, stripping down to his huge old boxers, covering them over quickly with a towel, then spending the following two hours getting burned to a more appropriate colour.

Usually when he sunbathed he fell asleep but today his mind was too preoccupied with the emergency at hand. He was insured, obviously, but it was not replacing everything that worried him, it was the uncertainty, the loss, the likelihood of the whole conversation with the youth being a carefully pre-planned ruse to steal a bag that was worth thousands and was the last of its kind. "I mean," Charles said aloud to himself. "If you are a thief targeting vintage fashion, Forte is the place to do it!"

Whenever anyone wandered out towards the pool, he turned his head quickly towards them, hoping to see the young man or at least a receptionist hurrying over to explain that someone was at reception and wanted to see him. But his hopes were in vain.

By midday the following day, all was obvious. Distraught and having made all the necessary calls to the insurance and credit card companies, the train station and the taxi firms, he realised that his mistake or not, the bag the youth had been so obsessed with was not going to be returned to him. He punched the bed and shouted out his anger. Shopping would be a complete nightmare here; he was three sizes larger than any shop's largest and he wasn't about to give any shop owner the satisfaction of telling him so. He could get the train back to Pisa to shop there or wait for the weekend markets in the small round forested parks with their miniature car rides and horse drawn carriages, but they were more often than not overwrought snatch and grab fights between locals and tourists with less impressive bank accounts, even though the prices were no cheaper than Harrods. The other option was to continue to wear and wash the clothes he had arrived in. He pondered the merits of each. Instead he unpacked the young man's bag and separated its contents into two piles; clothes he could squeeze into and ones into which he definitely could not. Then he sat down depressed and considered flying back home.

"I'm going to tell you this for your own good. You are fat, fat from all angles. You make pregnant women look skinny," his mother had told him during her final year. "Go on a diet or you'll die of a heart attack and now your wife has gone there'll be no one to find you lying there dead on the floor. You look a complete mess."

He stared at her in disbelief and watched her look away sheepishly.

"Well that's not Alzheimer's for a start you nasty cow!"

"Yes it is Melissa."

He stared at her incredulously. "You are aware you sometimes call me Melissa? Is this whole thing a bloody act?"

"Just get on a diet and find a new wife. I don't want to die knowing my boy is alone and useless."

"I am not bloody useless mother. I built a business empire from scratch that pays for this care home and for my ex-wife to live in luxury."

"She said you stopped paying her when your investigator found out she was living with another rich man."

"How do you… Has she been here?"

"She pops in now and then. What? We got on well. It's only you that didn't like her."

"Does she ask about me?"

"Never. Not once."

He growled at her.

"Yes, she asks," she sighed tiredly. "She makes it sound casual and polite but she listens like a hawk. Has he met anyone? Is he still fat? That sort of thing." She studied his face and smiled. "I'm only having fun with you, you know that don't you? Though… get on a diet, fast."

Charles held up a pair of trousers and squinted at them. They were a lot smaller than his own but the waist button could perhaps be battled closed or he could wear a belt, leave the fly open and cover it over with an untucked shirt. He dragged them up over the bulbous sections of his legs. To his surprise they zipped up with confusing ease; granted they looked like a second skin on him and the colour dazzled like a carnival but at least they fitted. He reached for one of the lad's shirts. Clearly the boy was not going to come and had surrendered the bag and its contents to him so now, with little choice, and no guilt, he considered the merit of everything he fished from it, the shoes, the stripy socks, the underwear, the swimming trunks… His own clothes, he suspected, had been dumped into a bin somewhere.

The first thing he noticed as he made his way into the bar today was the number of looks he was getting. Men admiring his clothes, women's gazes lingering all over him, especially around the front of the trouser which displayed him like some sort of 1970s porn actor. He had opted not to wear the youth's underwear, he was not liberal enough for that sort of ambiguity but now, self-consciously obscuring everyone's view of his privates with a dangling hand while frantically looking about for a newspaper, he wished he had bitten the bullet and put them on. Lord knows they were small and tight enough to hoist everything up and into a diamond crushing ping pong ball pouch and therefore remove it all from sight even if they would slice into his waist like cheese-wire.

"Oh my goodness! It *is* you!" the barman cried out with exaggerated eagerness, peering all around him as if searching out someone or something with overwhelming excitement. "I did wonder if it was you yesterday but you looked so different, so…" he pulled a glum face. "Well you look very handsome today you stranger you! Let me look at you." And stepping back, the enthusiastic Italian eyed the uncomfortable British man all over, then glanced up at his eyes with a grin. "I have not seen you and your wonderful wife for so long. I cannot wait. Oh I love your wife mister McBride. Do you wonder why I remember your name? It is because Eyes wide, because she has those huge, huge eyes, mouth wide, because she always makes us all laugh, McBride! Do you see? Eyes wide, mouth wide, McBride. Where is she?" "We are divorced. I no longer see her." The man closed down his excitement with the speed of a slammed door. "Oh dear, what a pity and she was so much fun. Now, a drink, let me remember, Black Russian, am I right?"

Charles nodded, then his reflection in one of the mirrors startled him completely. At first he was annoyed that whoever it was saw fit to stare at him so blatantly, then he realised it was himself. It came as shock. He barely recognised himself at all; he looked youthful, slimmer, dare he say handsome? And when he turned back to take his drink, once more he came across the lingering eyes of even more ladies who were not opposed to his noticing them back.

He took his drink to a seat at the window, drawing the attention of an entirely different crowd of guests who nodded politely while studying him as if he were a movie star.

"Surely they must have me mistaken for someone," he assured himself. "Either that or when I leave this room they will all wet themselves laughing and drop words like mutton."

But then he caught sight of himself once more in a different mirror and he tilted his head in admiration at what confronted him.

"This is ridiculous," he said a little too loudly and lifting his glass to his lips, shot a seductive wink to himself in the mirror. "If I'd have known simply throwing on different clothes made this sort of difference, I would have done it a long time ago."

He drank two Black Russians (three would be a mistake) and considered how it felt to be back in the hotel and in Forte without his wife for the first time in over two decades. Surprisingly, it was a lot less stressful than when she was with him. By now she would already have caused a fuss about something or other and opted to go shopping instead of getting drunk by the pool. In Italy, she became that overspending wife cliché, batting her eyelashes for comedic effect while acting completely out of control with her husband's credit card. He'd preferred her in Britain where at least he thought he recognised her.

A little merry and brave, Charles returned to his room, reached into the pile of clothes and pulled out the young man's swimming trunks. They were bright red, unworn, still with the label on them, practically a posing pouch with side straps so narrow they would dig a canyon in his side fat and make him look naked. He decided not to look at himself in them and tugged them up, grimacing as he shoved everything into some semblance of order down inside. Then, reaching for a pair of scissors, he tackled the excess of hair pouring outward in all directions.

Covering them quickly with the tightest pair of navy shorts that he had ever forced himself into, he cried out in exertion as he forced the button into its buttonhole and hoisted up the zip. These were so tight that his leg movements were forced into small steps reminiscent of the gold robot from Star Wars; it would take him an eternity to reach the beach.

In the lift, he studied himself in his old shirt, which now doubled up as some sort of poncho, then prepared to give himself a mirror lecture; one of those where he called himself lazy and fat and asked himself eye to eye what was draining his energy and enthusiasm and stopping him from improving himself. They never worked, these lectures, he didn't even feel guilty any more, just bored. He could change the subject with the click of his fingers and put the uncomfortable to the back of his mind without any guilt. Perhaps that was the root of the problem, his ability to discard the advice he needed to hear whenever he chose.

The trek down to the beach was irritating. Little steps with the fat of his inside thighs rubbing together and the flip flops slapping the ground noisily. He tugged his work shirt tighter around himself and ventured out on to the bright hot sand. The looks he got from the scorched zero-fat eighteen-year-old boys who took nearly a hundred euros from him in exchange for a square portion of the beach, told him what to expect from everyone else. A comfortable mattress, a huge umbrella, a little table, towels, a drink, snacks, ice, a mini-safe in which to store his valuables while swimming - anything he required became his. And so, shimmying down the newly acquired shorts, then tugging off his big old shirt, he revealed to one and all, his entire body clad only in a tiny red pouch.

The disapproving looks that had been offered up so far suddenly stopped. The whole beach, it seemed, was now staring and focussing completely on his body and his face, his arms, his hands, his belly, (even down there!) and with expressions of interest, not repulsion.

"Am I going crazy?" he wondered.

He had frozen, not knowing what to do in the glare of all the attention. A part of him wanted to put his clothes back on or hide himself with towels. He considered calling for wind-breakers or just walking in a straight and sober line to the foamy sprawl of seawater to submerge himself quickly under it - which is what, without a second thought, he immediately did.

The water thrashed and bubbled like champagne around his ankles, splashing up his legs as his big, hot, old feet sunk down into the cool, shifting sand. Grit swirled up around his calves and even though the water was shockingly, soberingly cold, he kept walking outwards up to his knees and then with a shudder and a "Jesus

Christ!" his testicles were submerged and he threw himself into the waves.

Charles loved the sea. He used to swim regularly when they had a house by a communal swimming pool. As a child and as an adult, throughout every holiday, if he was missing, he could always be found splashing about in the pool or the sea, as satisfied as a seal.

"At least I know where to find you," his wife used to tease. She wasn't much of a swimmer; when she wasn't out shopping or browsing, she'd sit at a table by the side of the pool burning beneath the sun, waving a cigarette and a cocktail, trying to look sophisticated and Italian. Sometimes Charles used to swim up to study her, loitering at the water's edge, his feet treading water, perfectly content to marvel at her beauty and her confidence. Towards the end he used to swim up to her just to put her cigarette out and flatten her hair with enormous splashes of water that made her angry.

The waves here could be ferocious but Charles loved the rough and tumble. He swam and bobbed and floated contentedly for an hour or so until he had drifted some distance away from his spot on the beach, then made his way back. Rising out of the water, his bulbous chest and football-bloated belly bounced above the tiny red trunks, welcoming the heat of the sun.

"He's single," someone gossiped. "He is staying at our hotel. Recently divorced." Charles ignored the whispers. Instead he quickly lay himself down on the mattress and called a waiter.

"I want a glass of Tuppapo - the diet wine," he told the bronzed young male model wearing dazzling yellow shorts.
"Tuppapo?" the confused teenager repeated.
"Tupp-ap-o - the diet wine."
"Ah Tuppapo!" He nodded unconvincingly and was gone, leaving Charles to flick through the complimentary coffee-table books and catalogues.

Forte Dei Marmi was now run by Russians, according to the conversations taking place all around him and most were outraged by it.
"They have forced out all the local designers so they can open shops you can find in any city the world over."
"Is he a Russian?" a voice hissed urgently in Charles' direction.

"No, no. He's British, divorced apparently. He's looking good for it isn't he? Some men just fall apart but..." Charles' forehead creased. He reached for his phone, took a picture of himself and looked at it. "I'll be damned if I don't look... not bad, not bad at all. Actually, in all fairness... quite sexy for my age!" he marvelled.

And he did; somehow and against all the odds, Charles McBride looked unrecognisably strong, agile and handsome.

The hours passed by lazily, sometimes in the sun, sometimes in the shade, more often than not, in the sea. If there was a pool nearer to his house, Charles began to realise, there would not be an inch of fat on his body. He made a mental note to sell his house and buy one with a pool or at least find a private gym, one that banned children and those horrifying people who swam lengths professionally and thought they owned the place.

As the afternoon drew to a close and unwilling to fight his way back into the tight, little shorts that restricted his movement, Charles covered the front of his swimwear with the bag he carried and made his way back to the hotel swinging his wet shirt. But as he walked through the crowded reception, in the equivalent of a thong, he reddened at his audacity, questioned his morals and slipped quickly into the lift almost tripping over his flip flops.

The lift was busy; three couples were wedged in with him, all silent and breathing at polite speed. Two couples were Italians he suspected, the other, American or British perhaps or… he jolted - a hand was resting on the curve of his bottom, squeezing it. Charles swallowed, never in all his life had he been the victim of sexual… well anything this exciting. He stood still, perfectly still and swallowed again nervously, looked this way and that, studied the four people behind him in the mirror but was unable to detect whose finger it was that now slid beneath the waistband of the red material and ran along its inner edge.

At the next floor, rather than anyone getting out, two more people wedged in. The group turned, adjusting their positions accordingly, so that now, standing at the centre of the lift with both arms raising the bag he was carrying, Charles was powerless to ward off any advances. He felt the hand return, slipping down his right side, pinching at the side of his swim-trunks, pulling them down a little. Wide-eyed, Charles held his breath. He was being seduced, sexually seduced; oh how many times had he dreamed of experiencing a random thrill like this?

Suddenly, the side of his shorts were tugged down even further, dangerously past his hip and the warm skin of a hip or leg pressed against him. Praying it was not one of the men, he marvelled at the gall and bravery of whoever was doing it. The men's hands, he now noticed with some relief, were all accountable, so it came down to either the redhead or the mousy blond. He looked at both in turn. Neither were giving anything away. Then suddenly, it all got confusing; his swimwear was tugged right down to his knees with enormous force and sharp, cold metal dug into him aggressively. He let out a cry of pain and alarm and pushed at the others to see what was digging into him. Reaching down to tug up his trunks, to the dismay of everyone watching him, he found, wedged down inside his costume, the slim, metal pole of a badminton racket hanging out from the side of one of the male's carry-alls.

The guilty party apologised profusely, moving backwards as Charles tugged the thing from down inside the leg of his trunks then threw it furiously at the floor. Covering himself, he slapped angrily at the lift buttons until it stopped at whatever floor was next and stormed out of it, disappointed and embarrassed.

After a shower, a rest and a recuperative brandy, he fought his way into a tight, white shirt that threatened at every button to explode, half-soaked himself with unfamiliar aftershave then wandered along to his favourite square - Garibaldi. It was the law, it seemed, in this part of Italy, to name every square Garibaldi but he did not have time to consider this further - his eyes had fallen on his favourite table being vacated at the al fresco café he automatically gravitated to every holiday. Squeezing past the tables with all eyes on him, he tried to ignore the bright welcoming smiles and women nudging each other then pointing at him. He sat down with a noisy outpour of breath, ordered a salad and considered the likelihood of the buttons on this shirt lasting for more than an hour. The material strained at every button, slid inside each fold of fat and revealed the thin white hairs of his chest and belly, putting him in mind of his impending old age, of walking frames and strangers who took damp flannels to old people who refused sheltered accommodation.

He fantasised about finding a reputable establishment that would take him in, dye the white body hairs black, not only on his chest but down below too and while they were on the job, shave off all the unneeded hair; God knows there was enough of that, his testicles alone could be plucked to make a full sporran. It was no wonder he'd never produced children with that sort of heat rising up every time he peered down his underwear. They could also sort out his toe-nails, his back hair, ear hair, eyebrows and tighten all the pores on his face. He'd sign up for the works. Such a mountainous task were all the jobs that needed doing, that they had put him off attempting a single one. He wondered how, as a youth he had always carried it all out willingly and with such attention to detail - even enthusiasm. Then he began to wonder in which year he had let the whole thing slide.

Wafting away the hot air and stretching his feet in unfamiliar shoes, he smiled to the waiter who put down the salad in front of him. Olives, tuna, rocket, tomato, cucumber, anchovies, so many fresh and healthy ingredients shimmering in the sparkle of the water bottle and beneath the delicious dressing. He reached out and had a nibble. It was more for show and to secure him a table than to eat. His restaurant reservation might be several hours away but he was determined to arrive at it ravenous.

With an irritable sigh, he ignored another woman smiling in his direction and turned to look out at the world's most beautiful people wandering around in the sun. Many of them were models, some were actors, others fashion journalists, paparazzi, designers or just rich people still searching for a table in any café to get out of the sun. Charles lit a cigarette and took a sip of his beer. All this attention unnerved him, he was not used to it, not used to it at all, but what was to be done about it? He could hardly stand and demand they stop staring.

"What on earth is happening to me?" he mumbled, noticing some newcomers who sent furtive glances his way. He flipped down his sunglasses.

The smells of pizza and garlic, coffee and sweet jasmine filled the air. His novel moved on two more pages. It was a dreadful thing about ghosts and crows and space travel that he couldn't make head nor tail of. He'd read the back cover six times to see what the hell had possessed him to buy it in the first place.

Beyond the canopy of flowering vines, under which he was sheltered, the sun beat down on the square with ferocious brightness, sending in wafts of heat and sedating everyone into a contented stupor. He suspected that behind half of the sunglasses, many of the customers were actually asleep.

One of the things about this little seaside town he had always appreciated was that the cafés were in no rush to turf you out then hand your table over to other waiting customers. Once seated, the table was yours for as long as you required it, it seemed, regardless of whether you ordered more. Life was calm. Life was good.

The younger man's tight trousers stuffed haphazardly with Charles' genitals cut into his sides like he was being hoisted up from a well by a rope that might give at any moment. It had been a miracle he had got them up his legs at all, let alone do them up. Reaching down, he popped the top button, felt his body cry out with relief and the weight of his elevated belly fall, cradling itself within the more generous confines of a familiar belt. His breathing grew easier and his face lost its dark red urgency. He popped a blood pressure tablet and one for luck then studied his chunky hands. He couldn't remember when he had let himself go. Had it been during the contentment of marriage, during the months they had hated each other and lived separate lives, cooking their own meals or later still? he wondered.

The last few months of marriage had been turbulent and unpleasant; each day dripping with venom and secret plotting. Once she had slapped him across the face with such force that it had dislodged a back tooth. He had pulled it out in front of her, shocked.

"Your skull and jaw are shrinking, because tooth decay is eating your bone," she screamed. "That's why your tooth came loose, because there is no bone left to hold them in!"

There was no truth in it; he had exceptional teeth, she had just been very precise with her blow. She was a very precise woman. He had stared at her in shock, his mouth filling with blood.

"JUST DIE!" she had screamed, bursting back into the room and attacking him again with her fists. "I wish you would die. Please God, let him die! Die now! Right now in front of me, DIE! Let me bury you in a coffin. Please just rot and be gone. DIE!"
But he hadn't, so she had dragged her heavy suitcases across the marble floor

in the hall, slammed the front door behind her and was gone.

"Perhaps I am not a nice man," he had questioned himself that day, rinsing out his mouth in the sink and holding his aching jaw. "Perhaps all of this is happening to me because I don't see how awful I am. Perhaps everyone else sees something different. Perhaps I deserve it. Lately I have seen no beauty in anything. Food is tasteless. I dread work. I dread coming home. I cancel every holiday she books because I don't want to be with her. I only see our friends because if you don't talk out loud regularly you'll forget how to communicate and become paranoid then go mad."

He took another sip of his beer, shaking the memories away.

"The last time I felt excitement or pleasure or fear in any form was…" He scratched his head but couldn't remember. "I think I might have died that day after all."

There had been the wedding, of course. That had been a great day, filled with love and excitement. Then there had been that trip four years ago, a year before the divorce, to Kruger in Africa. The safari, where his wife, refusing to believe a lioness meant her any harm, had leaned out of the vehicle offering it slices of ham she had secreted away during lunch. The animal had dragged her down on to the ground before anyone even had time to scream. It threw her about like a set of bagpipes then set to work biting and chewing. She survived it. She showed the scars off proudly at every party for the next six months, despite his interruptions pointing out that her actions had cost the life of a perfectly healthy but antagonised lioness.

"When you say that to people," she snapped in the most brutal of her 'quiet' voices, walking him through a cocktail party, unable to stop herself from digging her nails into his tender back of arm flesh that she wanted to dig holes through or destroy an artery in, "you make me sound like an absolutely brainless fool. Now stop it!"
"You are an absolutely brainless fucking fool," he told her with a smile, snatching at her wrist and tugging her nails away from his bloody arm. "And by the way, wearing that sleeveless dress draws

more attention to the huge flap of loose skin at your elbow than to your hunting scars."

"Charles! Yvonne!" They were already in a new conversation.

"We heard about you being attacked by a lion! Good Lord! You brave, brave thing!"

"She's the only woman I know who relies on others to kill for her," Charles told them jovially. "She brought the head home. It's mounted above our bed. Unfortunately we couldn't bring its children so I think they were shipped off to be fed by hippies with baby bottles." The stare she gave him signalled war. If he had been chewing gum, he would have blown it into a bubble at her. Instead, he listened to the polite laughter and her assurances that no head had been brought home then made his excuses and went to sit on a toilet.

Sometimes he wished he was still a boy, driving to the Cornish coast for a fortnight with his parents; they in the front seats and he in the back, a book of car games and a tin of travel sweets on the seat next to him.
Loud raps on the cubicle door preceded her nasty, shrill snapping.
"We are leaving. I will be in the car. I hate you. Do not talk to me."
He didn't reply.

He had taken a picture of her being mauled by the lioness and she had watched him.

A year passed by; she distracting herself, he plotting the inevitable divorce. During that year he worked such long hours and with such attentiveness that he accidentally made himself a millionaire, then a multimillionaire.

When he divorced her, he felt human again. He was forty-six, fat and tired but relieved to find peace. Life's new daily pattern was shower, work, home, food, sit and read, bed. Weekends didn't differ. 46 became 47. He met Matilda, it lasted three months, then Clarice, five months.

The Christmas he turned 48 he had sex with a woman in Pondicherry, India. She was bait in a police investigation trying to trap a cannibal known as Vincent Carbonara - seriously - not even a joke, but it had all fallen flat because Vincent turned out to be gay and was not interested in her. Then it turned out his victims were into being eaten and willingly offered parts of themselves up!

"The world is a crazy place filled with crazy people," she had told him in a bar in the old French Quarter. He was there on business. He had complimented her on her hair and eyes and within two hours they'd laughed their way through dinner, drunk three bottles of wine and she was on top of him naked bouncing up and down so aggressively he let out alternate shrieks of pain and fear.
"I have a foreskin!" he cried out. "It is sensitive! Please! Go slower!"
She continued just as aggressively.
"I hate foreskin!" she told him.
"Foreskins dirty, foreskins should be chopped off."
"I feel exactly the same about women who aren't circumsised. I mean what on

earth are they thinking with all those dangling…"

"You are a sexist pig!"

"And you are fat around the belly, it bounces like custard in a wrinkly old bag."

They burst out laughing.

"You want to marry me?" she asked.

"No."

"Why not?"

"You are ugly."

They laughed again.

"Ok my legs are getting tired and I want a cigarette, so speed it up mister," and she leaned forward, beating his big round belly like a drum, then ran her hands up her body, over her chest, caressed her breasts and throwing her head back, growled out peaks of painful, panicking pleasure.

Afterwards, in a bar, she bought more wine. "Please don't tell me your life story," she pleaded. "I just want fun." He clicked his glass against hers. "But you need blood pressure tablets red-face or you're gonna die."
"I know," he replied.

A year later he found her online and sent her a message, inviting her to England and offering to pay for her flights.
"Oh now you show up," she snapped at him from the screen. "Your son is nearly five months old."
Charles stared in horror.
"I am joking! And thank you but no. I do not want to come to England."
"I got the blood pressure tablets," he told her.
"Good, keep taking them until you stop looking like a blood orange. If you come

to Pondicherry we meet. If you don't, we won't."

He'd thought about going back but had come to Forte Dei Marmi instead. Fort of Marble it meant in English and the mountains were white with it, even the pavements were made of it. A waiter brought his bill at the wave of his finger and Charles uncurled some notes. The front of his own trousers had significantly outdone this waiter's, he noticed, with an element of pride.

Rising from the table he watched women's heads turn his way to consider him again - a rich middle-aged man in a younger man's clothes, alone on holiday. Ordinarily he would turn at this point, seek out his wife who would be hurrying back from the toilet, her pearls swinging, her face sandblasted, oiled, painted, smiles for everyone. But now he was alone; alone and happy with perhaps just a hint of loneliness.

Lorenzo's on Via Carducci, was, by far, his favourite restaurant in the whole of Italy; world renowned, Michelin Starred, book a month or two in advance as he always did. He had a different rule for eating here than anywhere else; he simply told the waiting staff that he would like them to choose for him, not to enter into any discussion about it and that he would be more than happy to accept whatever choices were made for him without reservation. Sometimes this was welcomed by the staff; sometimes it triggered the worried head-waiter to hurry over immediately to suggest that he… but Charles shook his head. "It is how I have always eaten here. It is how I always will eat here. Thrill me with whatever you are most proud of."

It never failed. His palette was tickled and teased, soothed and surprised and he felt almost drugged into a pleasurable stupor during his meals here. This request had always driven his wife crazy. She could not bear a meal that did not require at least twenty minutes of debate and agonising indecision, once the menu had been placed in her hands. Whatever she did end up ordering, they both always agreed that he had ordered, by far, the best food yet again, half of which she had eaten herself with her sneaky fork and series of apologies.

Emboldened by beer and wine and acutely aware that the entire room appeared to be watching him dine alone, Charles returned the smiles and lifted glasses to those offered in his direction, then he lost himself in culinary fireworks. Food, good food, had brought him to sensory ecstasy on very few occasions but he always hoped for it. It had happened in Roppongi, Tokyo with miso blackened cod. It had happened in Camps Bay, Cape Town with buttery lobster. And it had happened here in Forte Dei Marmi with unbreaded scampi, but not this evening, not in this strange mood.

The trouble with holidaying alone, he told himself, leaning against the statue of an elephant in one of the parks to light a cigarette away from the breeze, was the silence. It was not so much that he required conversation; it was more that conversation slowed the day down and made you appreciate things. Without it, the days just slotted together like a line-up of isolated events: dinner, walk, shopping, swim, all silent and all fast and all over with – over with because there was no conversation about any of it to keep it alive. There was no vocal appreciation in which you heard the tone of your own voice enthuse, no analysis to bring up the contrast of your new surrounds with the life you ordinarily lived or with other trips you'd taken. Perhaps his wife had been right about discussing the menu, God knows she had to be right about something.

She lived with another man now, a yank, a film producer; he made films for women. She had a cameo in one of them, alongside the actor Matthew

Mullane who slammed into her with a case on a busy train platform to get to the wife he hadn't seen for a year.

"'Ere d'ya mind?" she'd shouted in cockney, all shrill.

But he hadn't heard, he was already tongue deep inside Maxine Peake's mouth, their tears of relief pouring down their cheeks and on to the child he had yet to meet. A bubble of snot had come from her nose during the take apparently and they'd had to reshoot - Maxine Peake's nose, not his wife's. A wonderful sense of humour, very nice and down to earth apparently, again Maxine Peake, not his wife. Down to earth was important when describing celebrities for a lot of people he'd realised over the years.

He remembered letting out a huge sigh of relief when she finally slammed the door and left, despite his tooth. Whatever the divorce would cost, he had been prepared to pay double and when it had all been settled, there came, at long last, that much anticipated silence. He put the remainder of her clothes in bin bags in a taxi and took the rest of her things to a charity shop. It was over. He actually screamed "Woo Hoo!" and ran around the house taking a fresh look at all the rooms he would change the moment the locks were replaced. He slept in the spare room, called in the decorators, scraped away the frills and pinks then modernised every room. Had she been dead, Yvonne would have been spinning in her grave.

She called him a month later. "I thought we might meet somewhere neutral, to talk, discuss what went wrong, to get closure."

"I have complete fucking closure!" he shouted at her. "Don't ever call me again. We are divorced. We are nothing to do with each other." He hung up.

Yvonne liked control. He'd relinquished responsibility of everything outside of work to her so she could plan every last detail of their lives from the meals he ate to the way each room in their home was decorated. She signed his name on birthday cards, chose birthday gifts (even her own from him), arranged their holidays and days out, dealt with home repairs, even bought his clothes - it gave her purpose, while taking away his.

He plodded through her organised world like someone disinterested queuing through a stately home. There was nothing left for him to do other than to sit with her, agree and keep following her lead. That was how his attention to detail had vanished; she'd taken it away from him, detail by detail, day by day, year by year, meal by meal.

"Tell me you don't still hate her," his mother had pleaded on one of his weekly visits to her.
"I don't hate her. I stopped hating her when she left."
She squeezed his hand. "I just want you both to be happy."
"We are. I am."
"But not single Charles. I can't go to the grave leaving you alone and single."
"You're not going to die for years. Besides, I'm not just marrying someone

for you to be happy. If you die and I am single, I'm sure during the next few years I'll meet someone and you'll get your wish."

"Yes but that's no good to me, I want to see her before I die!"

"Mother, the days of dying wishes being granted went out decades ago, about the same time they standardised the size of headstone you can have in cemeteries even if you're rich and very insistent."

"I won't be getting the statue of an angel?"

"No, you'll be having the gravestone that's on dad's grave now but with your name chiselled on, under his."

She looked disappointed.

"You are a terrible son, nothing like my daughter Melissa."

"You don't have a daughter, you just have me."

She cradled his face in the curve of her palm. "My Melissa."

"I know you only do this to piss me off."

But she was gone, lost in some fog of confused memories and glancing up at him with a worried expression that told him he was now nothing more than a troubling stranger, too close in proximity. He left her quickly at these times, walking away before she could deny knowing him. It had happened before; it happened daily to thousands of other people in his position and nothing else cut as deeply as those confused tones that asked nervously 'who are you?', even though you knew the score.

When she did die, he fought like a man possessed until the angel was erected on her grave. Ironically, the marble had come from Forte. She would have been thrilled with that even though its face was a little… confused.

"The cross eyes are unfortunate sir. If you look close you will see it is simply a pattern in the marble, not the fault of the sculptor."

It was all too painful at the time so he agreed to anything. The thing was moved through the cemetery and put in place by a team of men who dared not look at its face when he was present. Now when he visited his parent's grave he didn't look either… perhaps one day he would laugh too or at least have it removed.

Stubbing out his cigarette at the elephant's feet, he made his way back to the hotel and swaggered into the bar.

Hotel bars, in business hotels at least, were usually knocking shops. The frantic congregated in them late at night, horny and drunk and ready to take all sorts of risks. This bar however was mostly couples. It was friendly and welcoming and reminded him he was on holiday, to smile, to have fun.

Two German couples in a corner were playing cards. He didn't think that people played cards any more, not since the invention of computer solitaire, but apparently it was still alive and kicking. He ordered a Black Russian from the flirty, overly attentive barman and took a table in the centre of the room. Ten O'clock. By eleven the place would be packed.
"This drink is on the hotel bar sir," the barman said, putting down a doily, crisps, nuts, olives and at last his drink.

Charles wriggled himself comfortable in his seat. It would be the last day he would go commando. He could bear it no longer; there were bits trapped down one leg, something else resting on sharp stitching, his testicles were overcooked and getting flattened… It would end this evening even if it meant wearing another man's underwear. When he looked up from adjusting himself, the barman and half the room were watching him with interested smiles. He frowned and picked up his drink.

At that precise moment, a familiar laugh set his teeth on edge, made all the hairs on his body stand upright like he was being electrocuted and he turned to see a lanky fellow in a stripy blazer, pissed as a sailor and saturated with panache or jour de vivre or whatever it was called, swing towards the bar with an overly-bright smile. He nodded to a bottle then turned, taking in the room, aware that every eye was now on him.

But it was not he who concerned Charles. Outside the door, a woman's laugh and chatter raised its volume, then the click of sharp little shoes hurried towards the door and suddenly, the barman who was standing before it, threw up his hands in excitement. "Hello Sebastiano darling. I am back!"

In a moment so horrifying, the most awful thing in the world happened to Charles, his ex-wife walked straight into the room. She gave the man in a stripy jacket a kiss on the cheek, took a sip from a glass of champagne then turned to take in the room.

"Why it's just as I remember I…"
Charles was staring straight at her. She now stared straight at Charles. For a whole minute the room froze as neither moved, nor looked away, nor spoke.

"OH YOU HAVE GOT TO BE FUCKING KIDDING ME!" he shouted.
She stared at him, not knowing what to do, a rabbit trapped in headlights.
"Charles!" was all she could muster.
Over her shoulder and out of focus he could see the barman videoing them on his phone.

This was not how it was meant to be. It was not meant to be at all - not ever. Charles was fat, dressed like a youth, his privates wedged everywhere like lumps of misshapen cheese and even worse, he was alone. Yvonne looked remarkably slim, tanned, her little summer dress clinging to her medium sized breasts that he immediately wanted to see once more. She'd had a facelift or peel or something, something that had worked and her hair was highlighted, styled differently; she looked incredible.

"This is the hotel I have come to since childhood. It is my hotel. I practically grew up here. It is personal to me. Why did you have to come here?"
"I didn't think you would be here."
"You don't think full stop, that's your problem."
"Now steady on old chap!" interrupted the man in the stripy jacket.
"You," Charles warned, pointing a finger at him, 'do not get to talk." He turned

back to his ex-wife. "Leave!" he told her. "Leave immediately."

Waving to the barman he ordered a fresh drink. He would not be moved, certainly not.

Yvonne turned to the bar, picked up a flute of champagne and knocked it back. Then picking up the bottle and pointing her new man out into the garden, she swaggered through the arrangement of tables and armchairs until she reached the man that had divorced her.

"I will not be leaving Charles," she said in a commanding voice. "So you can piss off!"

She walked three yards and then turned, grimacing at him. "And what the hell do you think you look like?"

The barman approached the table gingerly, placed the fresh drink down then looked at him, biding his time before speaking.

"I cannot believe you divorced her Mr McBride. She is…" he shook like someone experiencing a petit mal then threw up his hands. "You are so funny together!" He sat down on the seat opposite, much to Charles' alarm and annoyance. "Once you and your wife came to my bar, many years ago. You were both incredibly drunk and I thought, Dio, dammi un po di pace. Sono la madre e il mio rimprovero verra' ricompensato con le proteste al direttore, ma io devo rimproverarli" (Oh God, I am the mother and my scolding will be rewarded with complaints to the manager, but scold them I must.) Charles shook his head. "What?"

"You came up to the bar, loud and happy and making each other laugh and I thought the other customers would be annoyed with the noise you were making. Sai bene qual'è la reputazione degli inglesi in vacanza, e Signore, quel che si dice non è sbagliato." (You know what the reputation of the English is when they are let loose on holiday and by Jesus that saying is not wrong.)

"In English!"
"In English!" the barman repeated with a shriek of laughter. "That is so English!" Charles growled.

"You both quietened down, a little, and then you were so romantic together that everyone in this room," he stretched his arms out and around for dramatic effect, "everyone was spellbound. You said things to her that made this table say ahhh. She said things to you that made the men on the tables over there reach out and demand the hands of their wives and they looked at their wives with fresh eyes, like they saw them and fell in love again. I remember it was the first and only night that I cried behind my bar. I poured myself a large glass of wine and was given a verbal warning for drinking while working but oh Mr Bridges, it was worth it.

"Of course, then you finished the champagne and you were like this on the piano." He hammered his hands up and down on the table. "And your wife, she walk up to the piano looking beautiful and we all expected such beauty from her throat but she sung like… oh my God, it was awful, together you were so awful but everyone laugh, everyone laughed until we were all crying and then I throw you out because better to leave them wanting more but don't you see? You just need to see her with those eyes again Mr Bridg… tell me your name again?"

"McBride."

"Yes, McBride. Eyes wide, mouth wide, McBride."

"Sebastiano, she is with another man. I hate her. She hates me and…"

"No." He shook his head. "You hate her but she does not hate you."

"Sebastiano this is a private matter. I'd appreciate it if…"

The barman stood and narrowed his eyes at him, insulted.

"I apologise, I have overstepped the mark. I shall not be a friend to you any longer. And by the way, choose a leg; you put them down the right leg, you put them down the left leg, what is this?" he waves his hand manically. "I tell you what it is Mr McBride, it is a mess!"

Snatching up his glass, Charles wandered out into the garden without thinking. Fortunately it was large and sprawling, its tables made private by flowering shrubs and dimly illuminated statues allowing him to edge along into a cul de sac and not worry about bumping into her. He couldn't believe that she was there, in the same hotel as him, metres away; he couldn't believe her audacity.

The morning before she was mauled by the lioness in Kruger, he had loved her as much as he had on their wedding day but by the time they had set off to see the Big 5, he could no longer bear the sight of her.

As the lioness tore her from the vehicle, she had reached out, swinging her bag at him meaning for him to grab on to her arm and pull her back. But for some reason, he had simply taken the bag from her, thinking she needed both hands and let her go. It was all so fast and such a shock. As he watched her being thrown up into the air and slammed down, sometimes face first, sometimes back of the head first, held in the powerful grip of teeth the size of carrots, all he could think was 'why has she done this to me?'

The garden was beautiful. Tables flickered with candlelight, piano music tinkled from speakers at a barely audible volume. Warm, humid, air perfumed by the Jasmine bushes and the sound of the waves crashing on to the sand softened moods and made everyone feel romantic. In contrast, Charles wanted to drown Yvonne.

"God damn her!" he hissed to himself and tightened his fists so hard that his nails dug into his palms.

He should leave; if she wouldn't, then he definitely should, even if it meant she was turfing him out of his hotel. Anything would be better than bumping into her again. He smoked for a while then took a sip of the Black Russian. He'd ordered one in England and not liked it at all, but here, in the sticky heat, Black Russian was vodka and a coffee liqueur, it was the perfect drink.

Her laugh echoed across the garden allowing him to accurately pinpoint her position and distance. If he had carried a gun he would have tried to shoot her front teeth out.

In their apartment overlooking the planes of Africa that day, he had wandered out on to the balcony to shoo away a monkey but the thing darted or lumbered or both, into their room and started emptying bags and pulling out draws, presumably it systematically robbed every apartment this way looking for food. However, this particular screeching, crazy-faced vermin unearthed something that Charles stared at with mortification.

It had come from her handbag, she had obviously been forced to take it out at various airport scanners all along their journey. She was aware of it. A Rolex, one he knew very well; the watch belonged to his lifelong best friend

Thomas. Thomas had lost it several months previously. He had also become very jittery around Charles during the period between then and now, but Charles had put that down to the fact Thomas had suddenly left his wife. That had come as a shock to everyone, his wife especially.

After his separation, Thomas withdrew, pulling out of regular pub evenings with him, not returning most of his calls, he had once been at his home when Charles had returned early then had rushed off almost immediately citing some appointment he was late for. Eventually, when Charles did corner him and try to encourage him out a little more, he had looked guilty and whenever Charles complained about Yvonne in his company, he listened with clear irritation, never failing to defend her.

While she read in the bath, Charles dared to tap the password she didn't think he knew into her phone and within minutes a whole new Yvonne came to light. It turned out that she and Thomas had been seeing each other for almost a year. They both planned on divorcing and running away together. She had kept putting off her side of the bargain, mostly because she was not that interested in Thomas. The reason she was not that interested in him was because she was also seeing several other men; Charles' cousin Owen, his business partner Harvey, a neighbour, someone from her gym; these men came to his house in the afternoons and were gone by the time he arrived home.

Suddenly he remembered finding socks he had not recognised, though she had insisted that they were his and had shouted at him to put them on until had. He remembered bedsheets being changed almost daily, he remembered odd-job men loitering without tools, others hurrying away having giving quotes. And now, flicking through her messages, he came across accounts of his own lovemaking with her, explained in detail and with mocking dissatisfaction to complete strangers and even worse, to the men that he had always trusted.

She and Thomas and even his business partner, Harvey, had various derogatory nicknames for him. She joked about his performances in bed to them, gave various aspects of his lovemaking points out of ten, usually never above a two. And the men quipped back to her, joining in with the fun and insults, telling her to stop messaging them because he was there with them right now and the idea of him doing anything naked or sexual made them feel sick. Harvey had even texted back a picture of him, smiling with a pint and the words, it's not him who needs the beer goggles. As he read through their ridicule, he felt stupid and tricked and very alone, the shock and the hurt of it taking him so unaware that he could not stop himself from crying. He loved her. He had always thought that she loved him just as intensely.

When she stepped out of the bath and wandered into the room wrapped in a towel, he was standing with his back to her on the balcony, looking out at the fading light over the savannah, its beauty and excitement stripped away for him.

"Are you wearing that?" she asked with a hint of criticism and he had turned, nodded, told her he needed a drink, then kissing her on the cheek, left the apartment.

Before he had even finished the drink he was staring into, she opened the door to the bar and shouted over to him. "We are waiting for you in the vehicle for God's sake!"

Later that night, sitting in a hospital waiting-room while she was being operated on, he let himself into her laptop and uncovered picture after picture, sometimes of her, sometimes of the men she was sleeping with, sometimes both of them together; those hurt the most. There were pictures of her cuddling and posing with some naked man in his kitchen. In his bedroom, there was a picture of Thomas wearing his clothes with a pillow up the front, laughing while Yvonne cut up one of the arms with scissors. His favourite shirt; she had told him it had got mangled in the tumble dryer and she had to throw it out. There were others of her and some younger long-haired man sunbathing on the lawn.

Then he came across something confusing; pictures of himself, asleep, the bedsheets pulled from him, his body on display. In emails to and fro with her, Thomas had made jokes about his posture, some complete stranger called Paul had photoshopped a bra on to him, even Harvey had suggested she wrote names on his belly in permanent ink. He couldn't bring himself to read the suggestions for the words to be written on him more than once.

The whole thing confused him, the humiliation, his vulnerability, her betrayal, their hatred. He had been so close to her, to Thomas and even to Harvey, that he could not understand why the trio had turned against him with such vehemence. The bitter loneliness that followed, he kept hidden. A part of him wanted to ignore it all, to continue as if nothing had happened but every day that he left the house, he wondered who would be arriving the moment his car turned the corner at the end of the street.

Each day at work he moved with the efficiency of an army of ants, searching through every email she had ever sent, her every text, her every false profile on dating sites. He had hidden security cameras installed everywhere, made copies of everything on her phone and laptop, spent endless afternoons and evenings with a divorce lawyer. Calmly, he continued with married life, continued to work alongside his business partner, acknowledged Thomas, all the time marvelling that he had the restraint not to strangle each one of them.

Then, one day, when her email account fired off message after message to Harvey, Charles watched the man make his excuses and leave the office. Charles closed his eyes in dread and waited. Fifteen minutes later he got in the car and drove home. The bedroom curtains were closed, the front door had the chain on. The back door let him in and he crept, up the stairs, across the hall and paused outside the bedroom door, listening to her panting.

With a crash, he kicked open the door, stormed across the room and tore the sheets from them. Behind him some kid he had hired moved around with a camera resting on his shoulder, filming everything.

"What the hell are you doing?" Yvonne screamed.

Harvey was shaking. He became so white and petrified that he fell from the bed as he backed away from Charles who came down on the pair of them

with the stinging white flashes of a bamboo stick. Kicking their clothes into a corner and refusing them access, he screamed on the top of his voice.
"Get out of my house before I kill the pair of you!"

Harvey had run straight out of the room leaving everything, his keys, his phone, his clothes. He loitered out in the hall, realising he would need to come back to get them or walk home naked. Then Yvonne suddenly turned. She stood, naked, her hands on her hips, her chin raised.
"So what?" she spat. "So what? What are you going to do about it?"

The bamboo stick whipped across the backs of her legs until she screamed over and over. He knew it was illegal, he knew it was assault. He didn't care.

Grabbing her by the arm with a strength he didn't know he had, he marched her out of the room, grabbed Harvey with the other hand and shouting over and over "GET OUT OF MY HOUSE!" jostled them down the stairs, out of the front door and threw them on to the drive, slamming the door behind them.

On the security footage, he later watched them stand looking about, covering themselves, not knowing what to do. Finally, Yvonne returned to the door, hammering on it until an upstairs window opened and a set of car keys crashed down, scratching the bonnet of Harvey's car. Hurriedly, they got in it, though the car did not move for several minutes. It did not move until Charles came thundering out of the front door with a cricket bat. Then it moved very fast.

He didn't bring up the humiliating emails, he didn't bring up all her previous lovers. When she walked into the lawyer meeting with her rage focussed on just the one mistake, she and her legal brain sat mortified as Charles' representation read out emails, brought out picture after picture, including the one of Charles that they had joked and defaced and laughed at. She could no longer look at him. From that moment on, Yvonne could not look at a lot of people, including her lawyer and her family who had read what Charles had sent them via registered post with appalled expressions and open mouths.

Before the settlement had been decided, Harvey had resigned from their company accepting a pittance in payment. Then Yvonne called a halt to proceedings accepting whatever offer Charles had made. Charles was not interested in stinging her financially; his offer was fair but not generous. And then a day later he had let her back into the house to collect her things. She had lost her temper, screamed and shouted then had hit him so hard that she had knocked out one of his teeth, but you already know about that.

The waiter wandered over to the table and put down a bottle of champagne and a glass.
"It is from Yvonne," he said. "She wants me to tell you that she is sorry."

He nodded and watched the man walk away. A part of him wanted to hurl it across the garden smashing it into her table. Another part of him wanted to take it over and pour it over her hair but he had let go of all his anger towards her, so he picked up the bottle, went upstairs to his room and drank it on the balcony listening to twelve inch remixes of Chaka Khan on his headphones.

Yes, he was fat but he was a nice man, loving, generous, intelligent and well-read, with a good palette too, not as much of an income as he had once had, but enough to maintain a great house and take some decent holidays.

Down below, her laugh echoed across the garden again, a little more reserved, a little quieter than usual.

"There is one thing that I have not done on this holiday," he told himself, looking at the bedside clock which blinked midnight. Undressing, he reached into the bag, brought out a pair of the train-thief's black bikini briefs, tugged them up, snuggled down into them and wiggled.

It was an odd sensation letting your own genitals fall into the dents and impressions left by another man's giblets but it was not entirely unpleasant, particularly in a soft brushed-cotton. Over them he pulled up a pair of skin-tight navy flannel trousers, then wedged his stomach and chest upwards and sidewards into a little red number that would better fit a woman. Spraying himself from head to foot with one of the young Italian's aftershaves, he slipped into unfamiliar shoes then took the lift down to the lobby, practicing his smile in the mirror.

Two hours later, covered in sweat, drinking a huge cocktail and laughing with a group of youngsters who seemed to have adopted him, Charles danced to Scandinavian disco music in a nightclub that he had not been inside for almost two decades.

"My friend, he fancies you," a girl explained loudly in his ear, pointing to a man who was raising his drink at the bar. Charles waved back, laughed, but declined.

"I am not gay," he explained, shouting above the pulsing music.

"But this evening so many men here have come over to chat you up?" she persisted, shooting him a quizzical look.

He nodded. "I did not want to sleep with any of them either."

Charles did not fancy men, he never had, even though sometimes the idea of sharing a home and a kitchen, the lounge and the television and so on with another man made a damn sight more sense to him than doing it with a woman.

He had thought about it once, you know, giving it a go, but no, it wasn't for him. Charles McBride fancied women; he fancied every bit of them, it would be unimaginable to step away from that - and what for? Even during that game people play in which you have to have sex with one male, celebrity or friend or whoever, he had been unable to find inspiration and had chosen the presenter of Countryfile, the dancer one, because they would have got though it together with minimum fuss, apologised afterwards, shaken hands then moved on.

"You know," said one of the girls, walking with him away from the dance floor to a quieter spot where they could be heard, "you are a very handsome man. If you were not the same age as my father, I would be interested," she half-teased.
He looked at her and rolled his eyes "Get in line!"
She laughed.
"Angelique! Angelique!" her friend's voice interrupted them urgently pointing to the dance floor. "Listen!"
"It ees my song!" the beautiful blond cried excitedly, her accent suddenly heightened. She snatched at Charles'

hand and dragged him on to the dance floor. "This is me, singing, this ees me!"

The crowd surged up on them, jumping and dancing and gyrating against each other. Charles was swept up into the middle of it, drunk and laughing and singing and enjoying the hands all over him, right up until the moment the man who had waved to him from the bar, squeezed in front of him and pushed his tongue inside his mouth, kissing him passionately - really passionately.

Charles was outraged. Angelique was screaming with laughter at him. People were surging against them this way, then that. Humans of varying ages, twenty-three, thirty-four, forty-eight, nineteen, were bouncing up and down against his sides, rubbing against his back, they were on fire all around him.

Charles slid into abandon, "And why not?" he asked himself. "I deserve fun as much as anyone else." He tapped his pocket to feel for his blood pressure tablets, then jumped up and down with wild over-enthusiasm, like a heavy fridge being moved from side to side down a corridor.

At four am, the bar tipped out on to the cool, silence of the sands. Charles fell back on to a comfy mattress under an umbrella and made room for Angelique and whoever else wanted to sit. He watched the twenty or thirty other complete strangers lower themselves down on to the sand all around them. Everyone was relaxed, sipping water and chattering happily while listening to the sound of the waves.

Charles marvelled. He had done this as a youth. He thought these times were long gone but here he was in the middle of it, as drunk as he had been back all those decades ago. Granted he would pay for it the next day, but he probably had then too. He thanked God that no one had brought a guitar.

"Why do you keep saying you are fat and old?" Angelique asked him. "Too old to do this, too fat to wear that, you are not fat or old."

"Trust me, under these clothes, I am fat," he argued.

Angelique shrugged. "Fat is not a big deal, you should relax about it." She reached forward, grabbed either side of his shirt and tore it open, popping all the buttons.

"There, now we have seen it. Do you see that no one has screamed or run away?"
He let out a sigh and shrugged.
"Though, if you will just excuse me for one minute, I do need to be sick."
He kicked her with his heel. "What happened to my shoes?"
"I think you left them at the club." She turned and called out across the sand. "Hey has anyone seen Charles' shoes?"
"Over here," a male voice called back.
"See?" she smiled. "We all look after each other. Everything is perfect."

With a deep breath of contentment, the beautiful Swedish girl inhaled the sea air, leaned back against Charles' belly and studied her nails. "When I was a young girl I came here with my parents. My parents work in fashion, obviously. I was supposed to work in fashion too and I did, for a while but I didn't like it. I remember sitting on the beach, just over there watching the celebrities and the models and all these fine, beautiful women that my mother told me one day I would grow up to become and I always believed her."

"You are a beautiful woman," Charles told her.

"It's not important. What I am trying to say is that we grow up with all these ideas of how to judge ourselves and it's not until you let it all go that you find who you are."

Charles smiled, he hated drunk philosophy, it went on forever and got nowhere.

Someone wriggled on to the sunbed behind him, a male; hairy legs slid down the side of his trousers, while conversations continued around him.

"I don't think you ever find who you are because you are constantly in a state of flux," he told her, shifting a little for the male to get comfortable alongside him. "The only time you ever know who you are is when life stops still for a very long period and then, without fail, you discover you are someone you absolutely do not like. Everything is wrong with you, nothing is right and you're so disappointed, you don't even know how to do anything about it. Holidays, holidays are the way out of that. They have the power to shake your world upside down."

"And did you find out anything about yourself on this holiday?" the young man next to him asked, tuning into their conversation.

For the sake of his stiff neck, Charles did not turn to look at him. He shrugged.

"I think I found it's perfectly possible to still have fun, that I dress like someone at a funeral or at a tired old office and that I have a strong predisposition to forgive people."

"And do you forgive me?"

"Forgive you?" Charles said turning. "Forgive you for wha... YOU!"

He found himself face to face with the Italian youth from the train, the bag stealer, the wolf tail cutter, the man who let girlfriends put things up his back passa...

"You look good in my clothes," he said with a grin and suddenly the youth was hugging Charles, slipping down the mattress, resting his head on his shoulder and pushing Charles back down into a lying position.

Charles was confused. Why was he lying here like this, allowing some man to cuddle into his side like someone he had just had sex with and was about to drift off to sleep with?

"I want my things back," he said firmly.

"They're all waiting for you. I didn't even open the bag."

"Well that's a lie for a start because those are my shorts."

The Italian laughed. "I wish I'd brought your ugly old big blue jumper, I'm cold."

Oddly, Charles lifted his arm, pulled the lad into his side and held him close. Angelique, watching them with a happy, sleepy smile, lay herself down on his other side and cuddled in too.

"I suppose I should thank you," Charles said. "I also think I might have to buy you some new clothes because yours are stretched to hell and back!"

The beautiful youth laughed, shivering a little. "You can thank me on the train."
"Six fifteen?"
"Six fifteen. I have your return ticket."
Charles nodded, tugged both of the strangers in close, closed his eyes and fell asleep.

'Ladies and gentlemen, Please excuse my interruption but the train will stop at this spot for two minutes. If you have been watching the news and have followed the story of fat Charles…"
The Italian youth glanced sheepishly at the Englishman who looked sternly at him.
"then you will be pleased to know that this is the very spot where our hero saved his life and named him after his travel companion. Both of those

gentlemen are on the train with us again today."

A round of half-interested applause went up from distant compartments.

"Fat Charles," Charles closed his eyes, "is now reunited with his wolf-wife and their babies. To celebrate this and to help the Italian wolf charity WolfWolf, we are coming amongst you to offer you a commemorative issue of WolfWolf magazine."

The Italian youth grinned.

"I don't like you," Charles said.

"Yes you do. Besides, I want to come to visit you in London."

"I'm not letting you anywhere near my house, you'll bloody steal it."

"I gave it all back didn't I? Besides it is you that stole from me. You got up in a temper when I was talking about my ex girlfriend, you know the one who liked to do things around the…"

"Yes I think we all remember her thank you!"

"All?" he asked confused. "Anyway, you picked up my bag and stormed off with it. I did not realise until…"

"But you knew which hotel I was staying at. You even accused me of trying to seduce you by giving you my room number three times."

"I know, I thought it was a trap. I'm sorry. I was frightened."

"Oh shut up!"

"Anyway, you had an adventure!"

The fifty-year-old nodded.

"Ah yes, I must ask, did you have a homosexual experience?"

Charles thought back, alarmed suddenly to find he had - the man on the dance floor with the tongue and good God almighty, the force of that tongue; back of the mouth, round the teeth, over the tongue, under the tongue, all over the bloody shop. He should have bitten it, that's what he should have done, but then perhaps not.

"Hardly a homosexual experience, not sex, a kiss."

The youth looked disappointed. "One day. One day you will."

"You're obsessed! And get back over your own side! Sit up. Your legs are all over the place, cramping me in."

A few minutes passed quietly.

"So shortly we will get off and that is it, we will never see each other again?" the young man asked.

Charles frowned. "That's what travel is about. You meet people, you have fun, you wave goodbye. When you get home, the last thing you want is the people you met on holiday turning up, thinking the fun is all set to continue. People have jobs, slippers, soaps, their own friends."

"You don't have any friends Charles."
The words startled him.

"Hello gentlemen," said a woman in a pristine uniform carrying a pile of magazines. Behind her a girl-guide, or its Italian equivalent, jostled with a camera to get a good angle. "We were wondering as you are our heroes and our honoured guests, if we could have a picture of you both with the magazine? It's very special to us."

Charles groaned silently. He was hardly a honoured guest considering he had paid for the journey - twice. He was dressed in a lime green shirt, orange cargo pants and bright blue trainers. It was the only outfit he had not worn from the bag and he'd had it in his head to wear every single garment. Opposite him, the handsome youth was wearing an enormous puffy faded grey work shirt, nondescript black trousers and a pair of Loakes that were better suited to meetings or weddings. Both men stood, took a copy of the magazine each, turned it to the camera and smiled great big smiles.

Then Charles looked at the cover of the magazine and was furious. The wolf on the cover was enormous, its face was so fat it must have eaten every single minute of its life without taking a break. Its teeth, those that remained, were brown and crooked and oh for crying… for God's…

"It's practically cross eyed!" Charles shouted. "Look at it! Look at it! You named that after me?"
The youth was rolling on the seat, laughing so hysterically he could barely breathe.
Charles could do nothing but laugh too.

The train moved on, Pisa would be coming into view soon and the men were aware of it. Quickly the youth stood, looking about the empty carriage.
"Are you ready?" he asked.
"We cannot do this. This is ridiculous!" Charles hissed, staring up and down the length of the train.
"Now! It must be now!" And the Italian lad kicked off his shoes, tugged off his socks and unbuttoned his shirt while waving demonstratively at his companion. "Hurry!"

Reluctantly Charles stood, unbuttoning the lime green shirt, kicking off the ridiculously bright trainers, pulling off his stripy socks, then with a final look around, he shoved down his trousers and stood before the younger man in his minuscule and ridiculous orange underwear.

The youth in Charles' lucky green boxers appeared almost half-dressed just because of the sheer size of them. Their length was almost Victorian and there were enough swathes of surplus material to make an apron. The lad shrugged, peered about, then tugged them down. Frantically, Charles wound the clingy material that rolled itself into tight tubes down his legs, tearing out his leg-hair every inch of the way, until with huge relief they were on the floor in a knot the size of a pingpong ball.

Naked, both men stood before each other.

"Should we hug?" the Italian asked.

"No of course we shouldn't bloody hug! What is wrong with you?"

"You have a bigger… than me," he observed.

"Yes and you won't be touching it so crack on." Charles dressed frantically, falling back into his seat looking like someone old who'd forgotten all about colour.

The train curled through the outskirts of Pisa, pulled to a halt in the station and at last, both men stepped out on to the platform.

"So this is it? You don't want my phone number or my email or my name? We say goodbye and that is it forever?"

"Yes," Charles replied. "That way there is no pretence. It is what it is and what it was, was funny and interesting and very, very odd, but you are sixteen or twelve or whatever it is you are…"

"Twenty one,"

"Still a child, and I am an old man."

"You are fifty. Fifty is like thirty these days."

"You're sweet, stupid, but sweet. Besides you already told me I was an OLD fifty so damage done. Now we go our separate ways always remembering this adventure fondly."

The youth nodded. "Very well." He smiled and held out his hand.

"Goodbye Charles."

"Goodbye… whatever your name is. I wish you well in life."

"And you too."

Then both men turned and walked away from the station in different directions.

Charles stopped for a beer, as was traditional, at his little bar in Garibaldi Square. The owner was busy but came out for a moment, resting his hands on his hips to bathe in the last of the day's sunshine. He nodded to Charles and waved his arm out at the soothing golden light.

"It is a beautiful evening, so many beautiful evenings in Pisa."

Charles nodded.

"And this time you are on your way home to England?"

Charles nodded again.

"In several months I will see you again here for your four beers, two on arrival, two on departure."

Charles smiled.

"Is it habit or do you like my little bar especially?"

"Both," he replied. "But I've grown fond of it over the decades."
The man nodded. "So have I. Goodbye for now my friend."

In exactly three and a half hours Charles would be unlocking his front door. He liked Pisa, it was so convenient. Finishing his second beer, the fifty-year-old picked up his favourite Italian sports bag, emptied his clothes into a bin, then made his way to the airport.

THE END

About the Author

Alan Williams was born in Wales but has lived in Blackheath, London for a very, very long time. He's worked as a script editor for BBC comedy, edited various magazines, won writing competitions, has green eyes and yo-yo diets. When not sitting down, working, watching TV or writing, he is a highly sought after disco-dancer, award-winning kisser and is a remarkable lover.

Other Titles by Alan Williams

The Blackheath Seance Parlour

@Alan_L_Williams

32017359R00090

Printed in Great Britain
by Amazon